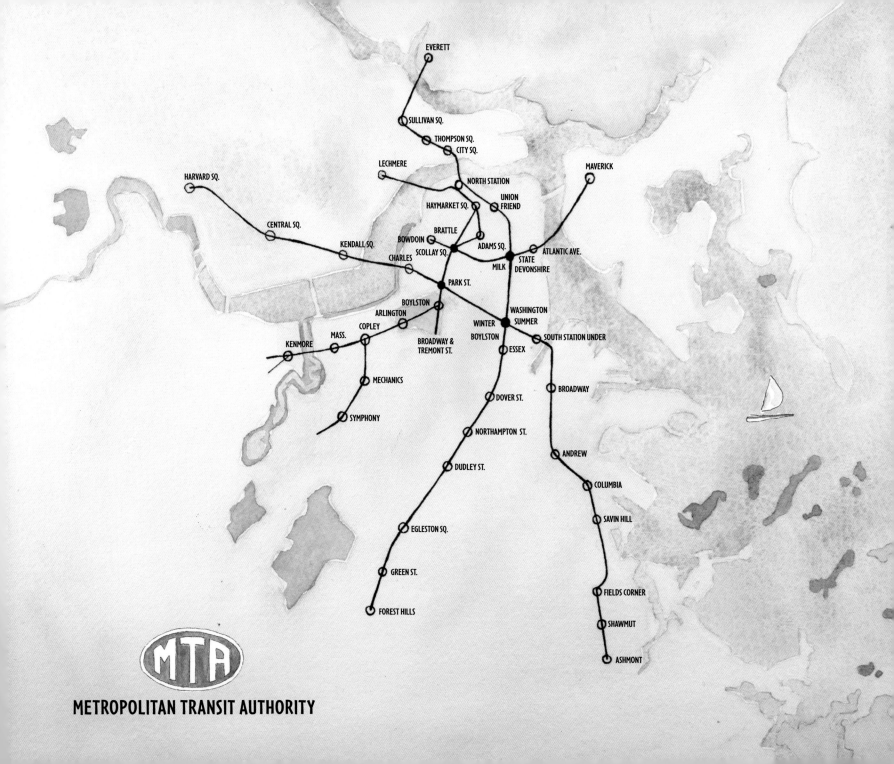

EVERETT

SULLIVAN SQ.

THOMPSON SQ.
CITY SQ.

LECHMERE

HARVARD SQ.

NORTH STATION

MAVERICK

CENTRAL SQ.

HAYMARKET SQ.

UNION
FRIEND

KENDALL SQ.

BRATTLE

BOWDOIN

ADAMS SQ.

ATLANTIC AVE.

CHARLES

SCOLLAY SQ.

MILK

STATE

DEVONSHIRE

PARK ST.

BOYLSTON

WASHINGTON
SUMMER

ARLINGTON

WINTER

COPLEY

BOYLSTON

SOUTH STATION UNDER

KENMORE

MASS.

BROADWAY &
TREMONT ST.

ESSEX

BROADWAY

MECHANICS

DOVER ST.

SYMPHONY

NORTHAMPTON ST.

ANDREW

DUDLEY ST.

COLUMBIA

SAVIN HILL

EGLESTON SQ.

GREEN ST.

FIELDS CORNER

FOREST HILLS

SHAWMUT

ASHMONT

MTA

METROPOLITAN TRANSIT AUTHORITY

Charlie ON THE M.T.A.
DID HE EVER RETURN?

JULIA M. O'BRIEN-MERRILL

ILLUSTRATED BY CAITLIN MARQUIS

Commonwealth Editions
Carlisle, Massachusetts

To all who share in the joy of singing "The M.T.A."

"The M.T.A.," written by Bess Lomax Hawes and Jacqueline Steiner
Used by permission—ATLANTIC MUSIC CORP.

978-1-938700-42-2

Published by Commonwealth Editions, an imprint of Applewood Books, Inc.,
P.O. Box 27, Carlisle, Massachusetts 01741

Visit us on the web at www.commonwealtheditions.com

Printed in China

10 9 8 7 6 5 4 3 2

Three dusty brown suitcases sat in the corner of the attic. They were right where my father, Walter A. O'Brien Jr., had left them many years ago. He started packing them before I was even born. He had packed them very carefully and neatly.

My father had not packed any shirts or pants or shoes or pajamas or underwear in these suitcases. Instead they were filled with newspaper articles, speeches, letters, and two old vinyl records.

The records were of his campaign song from when he ran for mayor of Boston, with the hope of fighting for the rights of all the people. At that time, the M.T.A. had increased the Boston subway fare from 10 cents to 15 cents, which for a lot of people was a hardship.

My father never did win the election, but I remember him telling me, "Someday, I hope you will tell my side of the story of the M.T.A. song—and these suitcases will give you everything you need."

It is someday now, and I am here to tell you "his" story.

So, grab your CharlieCard and maybe an extra nickel…just in case!

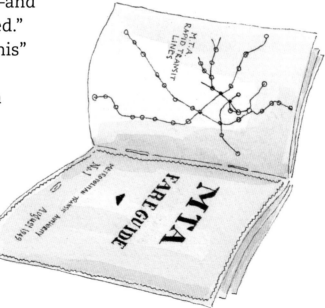

Let me tell you the story of a man named Charlie
On a dark and fateful day.

He put 10 cents in his pocket and he kissed his loving fam'ly
And he went to ride the M.T.A.

Did he ever return? No, he never returned (and his fate is still unlearned).

He may ride forever 'neath the streets of Boston; he's the man who never returned.

Charlie put in his dime at the Kendall Square station,
Then he changed for Jamaica Plain.

When he got there the conductor told him, "One more nickel."
Charlie couldn't get off that train.

Now all night long Charlie rides through the tunnel
Saying, "What will become of me?

And how can I afford to see my sister in Chelsea
Or my brother in Roxbury?"

Did he ever return? No, he never returned (and his fate is still unlearned).

He may ride forever 'neath the streets of Boston; he's the man who never returned.

"I can't help," said the conductor. "I'm just working for a living, but I sure agree with you. For the nickels and the dimes you'll be spending in Boston, you'd be better off in Timbuktu."

As his train rolled on through greater Boston, Charlie looked around and sighed.

"Well, I'm sore and disgusted and I'm absolutely busted. I guess this is my last long ride."

Did he ever return? No, he never returned (and his fate is still unlearned).

He may ride forever 'neath the streets of Boston; he's the man who never returned.

Charlie's wife goes down to the Scollay Square station
Every day at a quarter past two,

And through the open window she hands Charlie a sandwich
As his train goes a-rumbling through.

Did he ever return? No, he never returned (and his fate is still unlearned).

He may ride forever 'neath the streets of Boston; he's the man who never returned.

Now, citizens of Boston, don't you think it is a scandal
That the people have to pay and pay?

Vote for Walter A. O'Brien and fight the fare increase.
Get poor Charlie off that M.T.A.!

The M.T.A.

1865 Henry Clay Work wrote the song *"The Ship That Never Returned,"* about a worried mother whose son went off to sea.

1897 The nation's first subway system opened in Boston and 100,000 people lined up to ride.

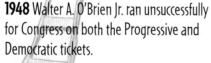

1949 Subway fare increased from 10 to 15 cents.

1914 Walter Alphonsus O'Brien Jr. was born in Portland, Maine.

1947 The Metropolitan Transit Authority (M.T.A.) was created to run Boston's transportation system.

1948 Walter A. O'Brien Jr. ran unsuccessfully for Congress on both the Progressive and Democratic tickets.

1941 The Almanac Singers (Woody Guthrie, Pete Seeger, and Bess Lomax Hawes) used Clay's melody and wrote new lyrics to support transit workers.

1949 Walter A. O'Brien Jr. ran for mayor of Boston with the Progressive Party.

1949 Jacqueline Steiner and Bess Lomax Hawes wrote and the Boston People's Artists recorded a campaign song using Clay's melody. Charlie represented the people of Boston against the M.T.A. fare increase. The song helped collect tens of thousands of signatures against the fare increase.

1949 On November 9 O'Brien lost the election, coming in last. John Hynes was elected mayor of Boston.

1950–1955 Walter and Laura O'Brien remained active in progressive causes for social justice, peace, civil rights, and the women's movement.

1956 Walter and Laura O'Brien and their two daughters moved back to Maine to start a new life.